KU-092-968

This book belongs to

DUDLEY SCHOOLS
LIBRARY SERVICE

Big thank you to Oliver Fuge, age six and a half,
for his dinosaur endpapers
C.F.

Lofty
Brachiosaurus

Scratch
Tyrannosaurus rex

Sniff
Monoclonius

DUDLEY PUBLIC LIBRARIES

L

742477   Sch

JYFUG

This book is printed on paper produced from
wood that comes from sustainably managed forests

First published in Great Britain in 2012 by
Gullane Children's Books
185 Fleet Street, London, EC4A 2HS
www.gullanebooks.com

1   3   5   7   9   10   8   6   4   2

Text and illustrations © Charles Fuge 2012

The right of Charles Fuge to be identified as the author and illustrator of this work
has been asserted by him in accordance with the Copyright, Designs and Patents Act, 1988.
A CIP record for this title is available from the British Library.

ISBN: 978-1-86233-826-5

All rights reserved. No part of this publication may be reproduced, stored in a retrieval system, or transmitted
in any form or by any means electronic, mechanical, photocopying, recording or otherwise, without prior permission.

Printed and bound in China

Three Little Dinosaurs

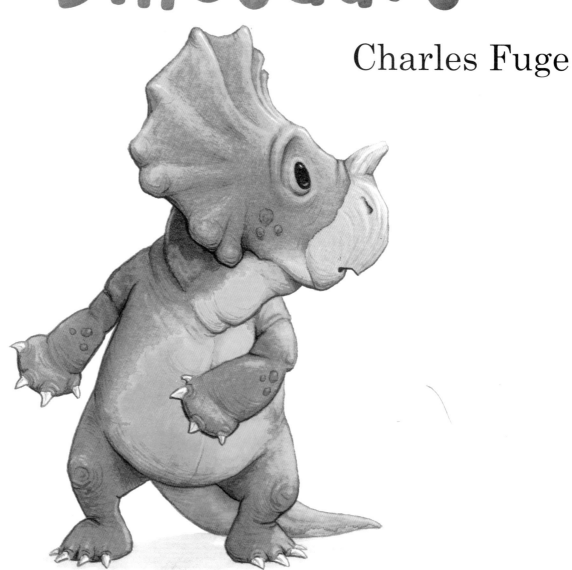

Charles Fuge

GULLANE CHILDREN'S BOOKS

Scratch, Lofty and Sniff
were the best of friends.

They spent their
days playing
hide-and-seek
in the forest,

or splashing about
in the lake.

Sometimes they
did cave-paintings . . .

but most of all they liked
pretending to **fly**.

One day Mrs Brachiosaurus was picking
pinecones for her famous pinecone pie,
when Lofty asked, 'Mum, can dinosaurs fly?'
Mrs Brachiosaurus thought for a moment . . .
'My friend Terry Dactyl can.'
'How?' asked Lofty, excitedly.
'Well, he finds somewhere high up,
then he spreads his wings, and takes off,'
said Mrs B.

I know a *really* high place, though Lofty,
and she rushed off to tell her friends . . .

It was THE VOLCANO!
In no time, they were
scrambling up the rocky slope.
'What if it goes bang?' worried Sniff.
'Well,' said Scratch,
'we'll just . . . **fly away!**
Come on!'

At the top, the three little dinosaurs
began to flap with all their might.
'Altogether now, one, two, three...

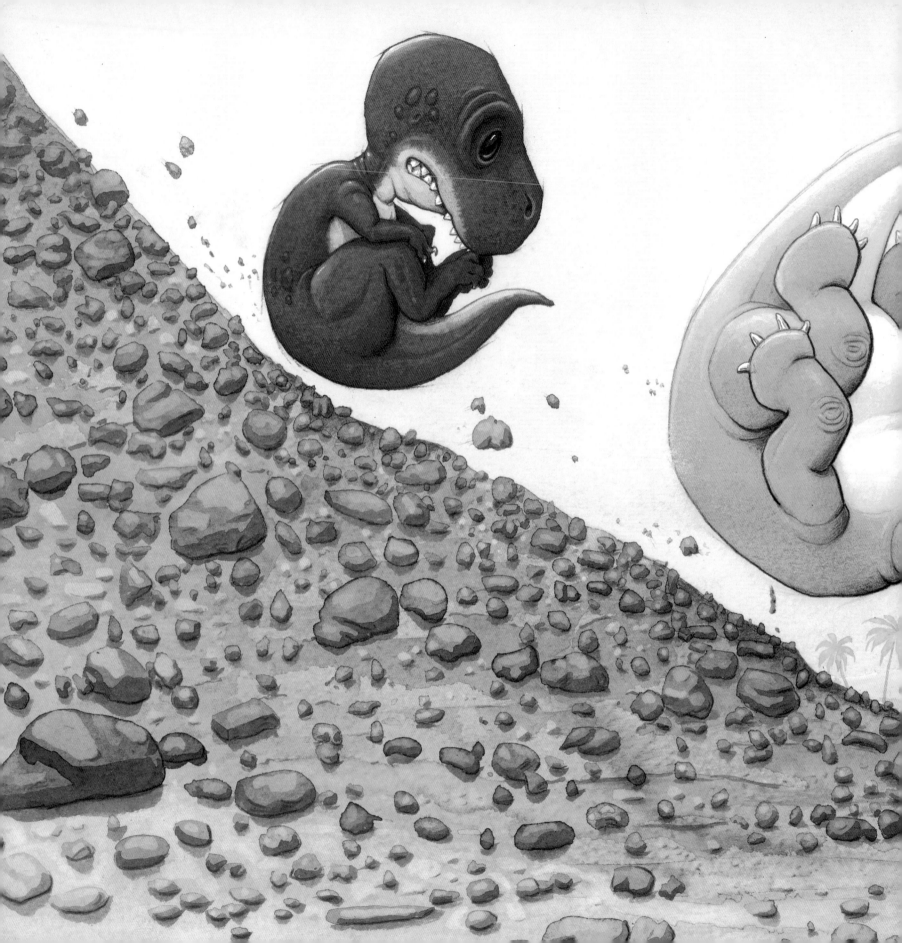

They couldn't fly!
Instead they tumbled head-over-heels
and landed in a crumpled heap.

OUCH!

'Dinosaurs **can't** fly!'
moaned Sniff.

'Oh yes, they can!'
came a loud voice.

'Who said that?' gasped Sniff.
'Not me!' said Lofty.
'Not me!' said Scratch.

The three little dinosaurs couldn't believe their eyes.
Above them, an enormous winged
creature circled in the sky.
'Wh-h-ho are you?' asked Sniff.

'I'm Terry Dactyl!'
the creature replied.
'Do you need a lift home?'

The friends grinned at each other.
'YES, PLEASE!'

So, one at a time, Terry picked them up
and placed them carefully on his back . . .

and they were off! Up and up,
through the clouds, high above the volcano.

'We're flying,' they cried,
'we really are **flying!**'

'There's Mum!' yelled Lofty.

Mrs B. stretched up her long neck, and one by one,
Terry passed the little dinosaurs down to her.
They slid down her neck . . .
whee!
over the hump of her back . . .
whoosh!
and
zip!
right off the end of her tail.

Mrs B. thanked Terry for his kindness
and gave him a large slice of pinecone pie.

That evening, three little dinosaurs
munched on pinecone pie and
watched Terry and his friends
swoop and glide over the volcano.

Then off to bed to dream . . .

of flying!